Dad

Mel & Tina

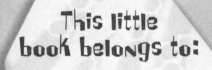

This little
book belongs to:
_____

alien baby

Published by Scholastic Inc.,
90 Old Sherman Turnpike, Danbury, Connecticut 06816.

For information regarding permission, write to:
Disney Licensed Publishing,
114 Fifth Avenue, New York, New York 10011.

0-7172-7743-7

Printed in the U.S.A.
First printing, November 2005

DISNEY's

chicken little

SCHOLASTIC INC.

New York   Toronto   London   Auckland   Sydney
Mexico City   New Delhi   Hong Kong   Buenos Aires

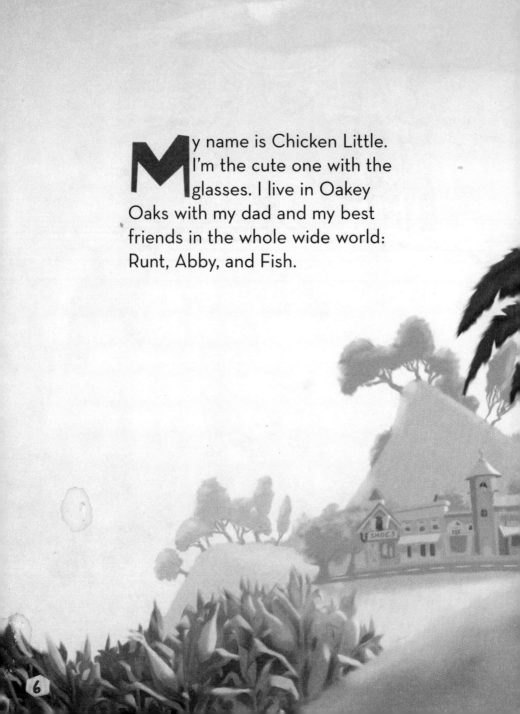

My name is Chicken Little. I'm the cute one with the glasses. I live in Oakey Oaks with my dad and my best friends in the whole wide world: Runt, Abby, and Fish.

One day, I was sitting beneath an old oak tree when—*Boink!*—something whacked me on the head. As I opened my eyes, I saw a strange thing. It looked like a piece of the sky.

I didn't want anyone else to get hurt by pieces of falling sky, so I quickly spread the news.

"The sky is falling, the sky is falling!" I warned the town, ringing the school bell.

Soon the whole town was in a panic!

But it turned out the sky wasn't falling after all. I had just made a mistake. At least, that's what my father told the whole town, when he tried to apologize. He said that I had been hit by an acorn.

After that, everybody thought I was crazy.
They called me "the crazy little chicken!" It made
me really sad, and my father just told me to stay
out of sight. That was the worst part. I think he
was embarrassed by me.

Then I came up with a plan: If I could do something spectacular, everyone would remember me for that instead!

So I joined the baseball team. At first, I wasn't very good. In fact, I was terrible.

But during the championship, I was somehow able to hit a home run! Can you believe it? One good smack with the bat was all it took. Wow!

I became the star of the town. Everybody wanted to talk to me and be my friend. It was fantastic! Best of all, my dad was happier than I had seen him in a long time.

"I guess that puts the whole 'sky is falling' incident behind us, once and for all. Hey, kiddo?" my dad said.

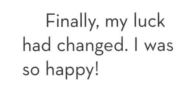

Finally, my luck had changed. I was so happy!

Later that night,
I thanked the stars for
my incredible luck. But perhaps
I shouldn't have, because one particular
star seemed to become bigger and bigger.
WHAM! It flew right into my forehead,
knocking me to the floor. Ouch!

"Oh no!" I thought. "A piece
of the sky! Not again!"

When I got a closer look, I noticed that the object didn't really look like a star. It looked more like some kind of panel. Then it did the strangest thing: It started to blend right into the floor!

Instantly I knew I had to get rid of it. No one would believe me this time, and I would be "that crazy chicken" all over again.

Finally, I called my friends for help.

"I'm sure there's a simple, logical explanation," Abby said.

"I don't care what it is," I replied. "I just want it gone for good and everything back to normal."

Meanwhile, Fish actually thought the panel was interesting. When he noticed a button on the back, he pushed it.

Suddenly the panel began to shimmer—and glow—and shake. But that wasn't all. . . .

The panel rose into the air, and suddenly Fish hopped on top. Then the panel began to zip around the room.

Fish seemed to enjoy the ride. But in a flash the panel flew out the window—along with Fish!

Abby, Runt, and I chased the panel all the
way to the baseball stadium. But the panel—
and Fish—had vanished!

Then right in front of our eyes, a giant
spaceship appeared and landed on the field!

It was unbelievable! A hatch opened, and two tentacled creatures came out and disappeared into the field beyond.

"C'mon," I said.
"Let's get out of here!"

But Abby shook her head and pointed to the top of the spaceship. There was Fish, waving at us! So instead of running away, we bravely ran *into* the spaceship to rescue our friend.

Inside the ship, I noticed a little orange furry thing. I didn't know what it was. I tried winking at it, and it actually winked back!

"Hey, what are you doing?" called Abby. "Come on!"

I raced down the hallway to join my friends.

Luckily, we found Fish quickly. But just as we were about to leave the ship, we discovered a huge map of the solar system. Each planet was crossed out with a red X, except for one: Planet Earth was surrounded by a big red circle.

"We're next," I whispered.

The aliens were obviously planning to invade Earth!

Suddenly we realized
that the aliens had returned
to the ship.

And when they spotted us, their eyes
turned red. We had to run really fast.
But the aliens chased us!

"The school bell!" Abby cried suddenly. "We've got to ring the school bell to warn everyone!"

We ran out of the alien ship and towards the bell tower, carefully avoiding the aliens' sharp, rotating blades. We didn't know that the orange furry thing had jumped out of the spaceship, too, and was following us.

When we reached the tower, I had terrible memories of ringing that bell. But Oakey Oaks was in trouble. So, once again, I rang the bell.

DING, DONG! Lights came on throughout town, and there was panic in the streets. The townspeople gathered at the bell tower. My dad was there, too.

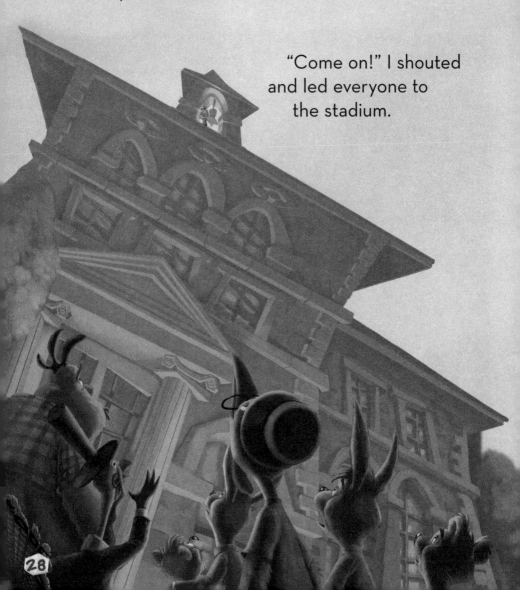

"Come on!" I shouted and led everyone to the stadium.

But the spaceship was gone.

"It's the acorn thing all over again," someone grumbled.

"It was right there," I tried telling them, "with aliens who are here to invade Earth."

But no one believed me. Not even my dad.

I was very sad. Abby, Runt, and Fish tried
to cheer me up. But it didn't help much.

Then I heard someone crying. When I looked up, I saw the little orange furry thing from the spaceship. At first, I was a little scared and almost ran away.

But Fish happily approached the creature and could actually understand what the furry thing was saying.

Fish explained that the orange
furry creature was just an alien baby.
He had been left behind when the
spaceship took off from the stadium.
Now he was lost.

But before we could do anything
about it, a terrible rumbling filled
the air. . . .

We looked at the sky and could
hardly believe our eyes. A fleet of
spaceships was attacking Oakey Oaks!
The alien baby happily jumped up and
down at the sight. He eagerly ran to
meet his parents.

For the third time, everyone in town panicked. But I knew it wasn't really an attack. The aliens just wanted to find their lost baby.

Just then my dad grabbed my arm. "Get in the car. We've got to go!"

"No wait! It's actually just a rescue mission!" I tried to explain.

"What?" he asked.

"Forget it," I said. "You wouldn't believe me anyway." He hadn't before, so why should he now?

Instead, I chased the alien baby. I knew I could stop the attack if I could get him back to his parents. But first I had to catch him.

Whoosh! A speeding car was heading straight for the alien baby, who was trying to cross the road. I jumped to his rescue, and barely avoiding the car, we slammed through the doors of the town movie theater.

My dad followed us inside. "We've got to get out of here!" he said.

"No, wait . . . just listen to me," I told him.

I was angry and sad, and as I turned to my dad, the words just flew out of my mouth. "You're never there for me!" I blurted out.

"What?" my dad asked, confused.

"I mean, you were there when I won the big game, but not when I thought the sky fell and not at the ball field." It was a relief to tell Dad how I truly felt. "You've been ashamed of me since the acorn thing happened."

"I didn't realize, son," he began. "I never meant to . . . the acorn, the sky . . . I mean, the whole . . . you're right," he finally admitted. "I'm sorry."

He hugged me really tight. It felt good, but we really didn't have time for that.

I showed him the alien baby. I could tell, he couldn't believe his eyes. But then he pulled himself together.

"Just tell me what you need me to do," my dad said. He was on my side now!

Quickly we ran towards city hall where the big spaceship was hovering. We climbed the stairs and popped the lid off the dome of the building. Dad handed me the baby, and I lifted him up into the air.

"Here's your kid!" I shouted.

Then the spaceship sent out a bright beam and zapped up the baby—and me and my dad.

39

Suddenly everything went dark. My dad and I were floating in some kind of chamber.

A deep voice said, "WHY DID YOU TAKE OUR CHILD?"

"I . . . uh . . . it was all an accident," I said. My dad tried to explain that it was an accident and we were just trying to return the baby.

"YOU HAVE VIOLATED INTERGALACTIC LAW!"
That sounded bad! I was terrified.

Suddenly two other sets of eyes appeared. We heard the baby alien babble something.

Then a soft female voice said, "Honey, he's saying they're telling the truth. It was just a misunderstanding."

"WELL, THEN—THIS IS AWKWARD, HUH?" answered the deep voice.

A moment later we landed on the floor of the spaceship.

The aliens were called Mel and Tina. They took us
outside where alien troops were fixing the town, putting
everything back to normal.

"I cannot tell you how sorry we are for this whole
misunderstanding," Mel told my dad. "If it hadn't been for
your son there, we might have vaporized the whole planet."

Soon it was time for the aliens to leave.

"Sorry again," Mel said to my dad. "But hey, I'm a dad. You know how it is with your kids. When they need you, you do whatever it takes."

My dad nodded.

Then as the alien family walked back towards their ship, a panel fell off the spaceship. *CLUNK!*

"There goes that panel again,"
Tina sighed. "Every year we come
here, this thing falls off." She pushed
a button on the back of the panel,
and it floated back up into place.

Dad and I smiled at each other. Maybe the sky didn't
fall on me last year, but it definitely wasn't an acorn, either!

As the spaceship lifted off,
my dad and I waved good-bye to the aliens.
I had a feeling that everything was going to be
all right. Now, do you believe me when I say that
this story is actually true—every weird bit of it?

EYE SPY

What a big adventure for such a little chicken! Look back in the story to find these out-of-this world pictures.